THE
SEASONALS

PAMELA JEFFS

Published by Four Ink Press 2022
Copyright © 2022 Pamela Jeffs

Cover design by Four Ink Press
Character Illustrations by Caitlyn McPherson
Language: Australian English

ISBN:
978-0-6453127-0-6 (pbk)
978-0-6453127-1-3 (e-bk)

Visit www.fourinkpress.com

For Anthony

Contents

Rise of the Seasonals

SPRING

Ruling Seasonal: Spring Wildcat

Origin: Planet Arbores

'Arbores was a verdant planet, with emerald skies,
raging volcanoes, and great pine forests that stretched
from the mountains to the sea. I miss my home.'

— *Spring Wildcat*

(10000 years ago)

I was not born here. My planet, Arbores, is far away, a broken world that orbits a dying sun—a home laid to ruin by the fallout of extra-terrestrial wars. We fought the World Eaters and won the conflict, but it cost us our existence. I know of no others who escaped the magic-wrought cataclysms— no others who found sanctuary on alien worlds.

I am alone.

And alone I work.

I want this new home of mine to be beautiful.

I navigate the rim of red sea cliffs that face south. Thin grasses cling to the sparse terrain, pressed almost flat by bitter winds that pound the coast. My breath, infused with a birth-given power to create life, curls across the earth. I manipulate it to build wildflowers and hardy cacti. I paint a sudden riot of colour where none before existed.

An old landslip cascades between two jutting rocks, providing a steep pathway down to the beach. I descend and sand spills away from my paws, slipping water-like down the decline. Below me, the tide has left piles of silvered driftwood banked against the base of the towering cliffs. Some yellow and green, I decide, would work well to brighten it there. So, I breathe again. Paper daisies spring to life amongst the dead boughs and rocks, tiny heads dancing like suns in the salty breeze.

But one section remains bare. I frown and try again.

Nothing blooms in that place.

Strange.

I snuff the air. The feeble scent of unnatural decay catches in my throat.

My hackles rise.

The smell is familiar.

I circle a haphazard lay of weathered logs. Behind it emerges a jagged cleft, the opening ink-dark. I ease closer and the odour grows stronger. The threshold, I note, is stained black and is littered with clotted clumps of dried kelp. Scattered amongst it are the small skeletons of birds and other half-rotted carcasses of lizards. Blue stars—soul-lights—hover over the remains. My top lip wrinkles.

Power that ties souls to their bones—I encountered it during the wars on my home planet. Such magic belongs to *things* born in the airless oceans of space: creatures that consume the living.

World Eaters.

Dread settles along my spine. I thought we had killed them all. Our planet was sacrificed with that aim. Perhaps one escaped. I approach the flotilla of soul lights. The skeletons below them are incomplete. Frustrated, I growl, low. Rebuilding flesh and reanimating it is within my power, but the outcome is uncertain without a full base structure to build upon. I can't help these small beings back to their previous lives, but I can at least grant them freedom. My breath warms the air and I let my gift sever the foul magic's connections. The souls fly free.

My attention returns to the cleft. I slip inside, padded footsteps silent. Cold stone closes around me and the sound of waves recedes. My heart beats an uneasy tattoo—a rhythm underpinned by a fear-wrought bass line. I edge along the snaking path. Old memories replay in my mind—the corpses of wildcats, my brothers and sisters, souls tied to their skeletons. I released those I could before Arbores fell but I was only one and there were many. I failed to free them all.

The guilt remains always.

The gloom lightens, burned away by a growing green light. The passage peters out. Beyond, a sea cave emerges, salt-slick walls rugged and illuminated by phosphorescence.

And there I find my enemy. The World Eater slumbers in a shallow pool of fouled seawater near the centre of the cave. Its mountainous cephalopod body reeks of death. Its translucent green flesh flickers with blue-black light—soul lights consumed and mutated to feed the creature's terrible power.

I can't let another world die to this creature's appetites. Gently, I coax the lank seaweed, floating on the surface of the pool, to life. The strands shudder and swell. Inch by inch I lengthen them and coil the threads into ropes. The World Eater shifts, but remains asleep. I send the straps rising to bind the monster.

The World Eater's lidless eyes snap to awareness, two bright-yellow orbs split by thick, black, pupils. Confused, the creature coughs a wordless cry of outrage. Its tentacles strain against the bonds, snapping several with a sharp crack.

'Desist!' I snarl.

And the creature swivels.

'Wildcat survivor,' it says, its voice spitting like a boiling sun. 'Release me.'

'I will not,' I say.

The light beneath the creature's skin pulses faster.

'You want me dead?' it growls. 'Will you scorch this world bare like your own to see it done?'

'Never.'

'Then you must release me, for you will never contain me.'

'I'll stop you.'

The creature laughs. Its great sack-like brain jiggles. 'You haven't the stomach for killing,' it says, 'otherwise I'd already be dead.'

I hesitate. The monster's right.

The World Eater scoffs, a burbling sound. 'You're pathetic and you'll die just like the last wildcat who tried to stop me.'

Its sly eyes flick to the back corner of the cave. I risk a glance. A glint of light catches off the rounded edges of golden bones and a huge feline skull.

Not from this world.

Sudden grief and anger stagger me. Another wildcat? Here on Earth?

But slain.

There is time neither to grieve nor to investigate. The creature tenses and its remaining bindings bulge and then shear apart. One long tentacle flicks out and catches me across the cheek. The suckers slip off my fur but the force of the blow knocks me to the ground. I taste blood.

Another tentacle flicks wide.

I strike.

Claws and teeth connect with gelatinous flesh. Malodourous black ink floods across my back and neck. Its acid composition scorches me in a slick of agony. My grip loosens and the monster slithers free.

I rally. I slice. I miss.

Desperate, I cough and life responds.

Wild grape vines erupt from the walls and slither across the floor. They wind around the creature's bulbous head and contract. Long-needled cacti burgeon from the ground, their stout and weaponed limbs impaling flailing tentacles.

The creature cries out. Its eyes then illuminate, glowing a venomous gold. Its body ripples and blue-black electricity gathers at the tip of each free tentacle.

My vines and cacti wilt as the World Eater's foul energy feeds off their life forces.

Lightning cracks from its limbs and bounds off the salt-slick stone walls. The burning snarls of light whip back and encompass my torso, tethering me to their firestorm touch. My fur singes. Overpowered by the smell and the pain, I gag and struggle, haunches bunched and teeth gritted.

I take a sobbing breath, and call to me the roots of dune grasses. But my gentle magic fails in the grip of the creature's raw power.

My bones creak, and then crack. My soul slips in my skin as the monster tries to draw it out of me. Soon I'll lie alongside my sibling.

Sibling.

Of course.

With a last surge, I gather my failing magic and breathe out one last time. I send my remaining power careening across the cavern to settle on the golden bones of the other wildcat. I don't know if a full base structure lies there, I don't know what will emerge if it doesn't, but this is my only chance, and Earth's chance also.

The skeleton shudders. Flesh forms over it, blood vessels, and a heart to beat life into new limbs.

The monster's attention slips to the wall.

Something rises where only bones existed before, a form half-revealed in the rippling light cast by the World Eater's power. I can't make out the shape. Is that the dappled white-gold coat of a wildcat?

The creature's grip tightens and my vision blurs.

Darkness descends.

***

I'm not sure how long I linger untethered. Minutes? Centuries? Time feels irrelevant. But consciousness does return, and with it hope that I still live. First, I hear the faintest of sounds—the calls of the gulls and the roar of the waves. Then pain follows, insistent, bright, and sharp-edged.

And heat—

A blistering heat.

I open my eyes to a maelstrom of fire.

An unfamiliar life form stands beside me. Blonde-haired and without fur, she balances upright on two muscular legs. Flames roar like a torrent from her twin slender hands. But the power gutters and rallies as if she is unfamiliar with the wielding of it. Her eyes blaze blue as a summer sky. They follow shadows that lurch in the inferno opposite. I make them out—tentacles and a great sack-like brain surrounded by a force-field of blue-black light.

The World Eater.

My protector's legs tremble. She slumps to her knees and her fire dims. The World Eater roars and whips out a tentacle. Primal instinct takes over. I hurl myself between the monster and the female. My blistered skin cracks and every bone in my body aches. I gather breath into tortured lungs and breathe out a monsoon. My power circles the cavern, gathering seaweed and dune grass roots. I coil them into ropes, thicker than my waist. With a desperate cry, I wrap the length around the creature's neck.

The World Eater's eyes bulge. Lightning blisters from the tips of its tentacles but fizzles out mid-air. I squeeze tighter again, grinding my teeth. Finally, the cephalopod slumps into unconsciousness.

I know I should end it, but the creature was right. I can't kill. I let the ropes around the monster's neck loosen. The female gets back to her feet and pushes past me. Her skin is hot, like lava. Fire ignites in her palm. She glances back, her eyes catching mine for a moment. I'm not sure if it's pity or chastisement colouring her gaze. Then she turns to the monster. Her power, stable for the moment, roars outward. The cave floor collapses into slag and disappears out from under the World Eater.

The creature falls, swallowed whole into a crevasse now stretching past us and out toward the beach. The female looks back at me, shoulders heaving and breaths ragged. Her hands die to glowing embers.

'Hello, Brother,' she says.

***

My sister is not what she once was, but she is perfect in her new form.

'Is this Arbores?' she asks.

'No,' I say. 'A different world. A planet called Earth.'

She holds up her new hands and flexes her fingers. 'This isn't my body.'

'No. Your skeleton was incomplete. My magic reshaped you into this form.'

Her delicate chin tilts. 'This new configuration is adequate.'

Then her gaze grows grim.

'I recall everything ending. I fell through the universe. I landed … Something … found me.' Her eyes flick to the crevasse.

'The World Eater killed you,' I reply, confirming her unspoken suspicion.

'And your power returned me?'

'Yes.'

'That is a fine gift to have been born with.'

'It has its uses.'

My sister points to the crevasse. 'That thing in there. It should be finished.'

'I create life,' I say. 'I cannot end it.'

My sister frowns. 'Then my power must keep it imprisoned.'

'Can it do that?'

She holds up her hand and her fingers draw sparks from the air. 'My gift is immortal fire, Brother. But it must align with the rhythms of a world's four seasons, to create an absolute barrier. This crevasse—the Line—will hold all our enemies as long as we maintain the natural balances of this world.'

'Will it hold other World Eaters if they come?' I ask.

'Yes. But to do so would mean commitment to the service for eternity.'

'Earth is worth the sacrifice.'

My sister tosses her hair back over her shoulder. 'Show me.'

'Come,' I say.

I lead my sister out of the cave and onto the beach. We are met with dusk and a red sky. Her eyes widen.

'It's so different from home. So beautiful.'

'Will you help me protect it?'

Her clear blue gaze turns to mine. 'We are only two where four are needed for such a duty—one to oversee each of the world's seasons. Who would help us?'

'Human civilisations exist to the north and south. Perhaps we start our search there.'

My sister looks out across the ocean. For long moments, she takes in the splendour of dusk, the half-fallen disk of the sun spilling gold against the roiling whitecaps.

'All right, Brother. We become Seasonals then. Protectors of Earth.'

She points to the horizon. 'The lands behind the sun call to me. I shall preside over summer from there and guard the Line for that season.'

The Lands behind the Sun. I think on those great expanses of sand running on forever—the perfect habitat for a creature of fire.

'I will remain here in the south,' I say. 'My gift best suits spring.'

My sister nods, as if the choice is an obvious one. 'Only autumn and winter left, then, to secure.' She turns. Her smile is jewel-bright. 'We have work to do.'

'We do, Sister.'

She winks. 'Call me Summer Maiden. We will name you Spring Wildcat.'

'That is a good name,' I say, my heart full in her presence.

It's good to no longer be alone.

Battle at the Line

SUMMER

Ruling Seasonal: Summer Maiden

Origin: Planet Arbores

'Sacrifice and dedication to duty are both the stones
and the thorns that line a warrior's path.'

— *Summer Maiden*

(2000 years ago)

This land behind the sun, my land, is a continent of fire and light. The desert extends from horizon to horizon, a wind-rippled ocean of bone-white sand. The colour echoes the tone of my skin, pale and delicate. But do not be deceived. This land, like me, is for the hard, the brave, and the indomitable. And even though I come from a different world—a place that birthed me from the heart of a volcano—this is my home. I am fire and strength and that power flows through the blood of my people. I am their mother and the symbol of their immortal souls.

I am Summer Maiden.

The dry, hot breeze rises, coiling around me and carrying with it the rich perfumes of faraway places. My fingers curl tighter on the crow's nest railing as I lean into the scents with delight—the rich aromas of the northern islands: roasting fish, salted dates, and the sweet-rot smell of spring days dying.

The summer solstice approaches.

Another month and my brother, Spring Wildcat, will retire to his fair southern beaches and it will be my turn to watch over this world again.

The teasing breeze twists in a sudden flurry. My loose curls roll against my breast. I grasp the sandspider ropes, ready to leave my position, but something more than scents ride the wind.

A distant sound.

Slither. Slice. Snarl—

The echo of a scream.

My brow furrows.

'Wildcat?' I mutter. He is heading back early. Why? But deep down, I already know. Since the time we became Seasonals to protect Earth, the industry of humans has grown. Climates are changing and the lengths of our seasons have shortened.

'Curses,' I snarl. I clench my teeth and swing down to the deck. The tough sandspider silk ropes slide through my palms. My bare feet hit the opaque deck with a thump.

'Daughters! To your stations!' I yell. 'Make ready the sails. We head to the Line!'

'So early?' asks my first mate, Krysanthe.

I frown. 'Far too early.'

My crew, warrior women of stature and strength, run the length of the deck, preparing my glass galleon for travel. The supple whale skin sails drop from their bindings and billow wide, catching the superheated currents in their grasp. The hides, gifted by the whale-folk from the cold southern oceans, glisten silver in the blue-white light. The great metal sleds below the hull creak as they lean into the blistering white dune sea.

I enter my cabin. Charts spill across my desk. I dig through them, searching for the one denoting the distance to the southern end of the Line. I find it at the bottom of the stack. The rich map, inked in ultramarine and gold, holds no fair news.

We are at least a half-day sail away from my brother.

And from the monsters that hunger for him.

For a moment, my heart tightens. Some of those creatures imprisoned in the Line were once my children. Spring Wildcat used his power over life to create them for me when I first came to these lands. Immortal eagles of summer. Jewels of the sky. But as with all things, time corrupts, and I was forced to bind them to the darkness. I shudder and push away such memories. Outside, my daughters begin to sing the wind to rising. I must get to Wildcat in time to help him cross. There is no choice. We Seasonals are all needed to maintain the power holding the Line. For more than just my eagles live within it. The magic also holds world-eating monsters at bay.

If Wildcat falls, we all do.

***

We approach the Line with the sinking of the sun. White sand gives way to a broken-edged ridge of volcanic rock. Dusk's deep golden light catches the edges of the stone, sending splinters of shadow sailing toward the east. I signal to my first mate and the sand anchor is released. It catches and the sleds groan as we draw to a halt.

The Line is a jagged cleft I carved into the planet's bedrock long ago. From it emanate cries of despair and longing—of terror and wicked desire.

My shoulders clench around the unnatural din. Again, I lament the fate of my lost children.

Krysanthe approaches, her copper hair like fire in the light. She holds my fire-forged blade.

'Give them hell, Mother,' she says.

'I would my child, but they're already there. We'd do better to wish them peace.'

Krysanthe nods and presses the sword to my hand. 'Then dispatch them swiftly. Don't let them suffer.'

***

Wildcat's snarl echoes from the near distance, a sound like steel shearing. I gather the fading fire of the sun's light and craft a skiff to carry me. I float up and away from the deck, across my ship's rails. The remnant heat rising from the sand below holds me aloft.

With a twist of my wrist, my tiny vessel surges forward. I speed toward the sound of my brother, holding close to the Line—but not too close; I do not wish to tempt the creatures reaching up from the dark.

The wind whispers, carrying a warning of what lingers just beyond the horizon. I clutch my sword close. The clamour of battle grows louder.

The skyline shatters into a sudden, uneven contour. Silhouettes of colossal tentacles burst up from the Line, writhing, shifting, and coalescing. Their poisonous tips rise and fall, stabbing—sharp and sudden. My heart withers. It's the most dangerous of monsters that has risen this turn of the season. My brother battles none other than the dreaded World Eater.

Spring Wildcat struggles in the monster's grip. Muscled, taloned, and determined. His gold and white spotted fur is dark with sweat and marred with blood. A scarred muzzle wrinkles back as he roars, long teeth glittering.

Wildcat's head snakes forward and tears into a tentacle. An unearthly scream blisters up from the cleft. Violet blood sprays the rock and a bitter stench fills the air. The tentacle shudders then tightens. The creak of Wildcat's bones is like boulders breaking.

My brother rallies and strikes again. More blood. More screams.

I leap from my skiff. The vessel dissipates into a shower of sparks, the gathered light released. I land, sword bared to hack at the dire tentacles. They fall around me, slabs of dying flesh. The World Eater's arms recoil from the touch of my steel, the fire and heat in the metal anathema to all creatures of the dark.

Wildcat snarls somewhere in the melee. I've lost him in the mass of writhing flesh.

'I am coming, Brother,' I call out, my voice bright-edged with power so it can carry.

A snarl rolls out in response, half sob, half hope.

I cut and cut again, winning each step with the slaughter of wicked flesh. Acidic slime rains down from the tentacles thrashing high above, matting my hair to my shoulders. My skin burns in a thousand places.

Seconds turn to minutes.

I reach the epicentre.

Wildcat is pinned to the blasted earth, glowing blue eyes desperate. He struggles to gain his feet, claws scrabbling against the rock but finding no purchase. I surge forward, sword raised. It falls and falls again, but somehow seems to have lost its edge. Then I see why. Tentacles are suckered to a weeping wound on Wildcat's chest. The creature is feeding on his life force. My blade cannot hurt my kin and with part of Wildcat's soul consumed, the beast has claimed immunity.

I reach Wildcat, despairing at his injury. My stomach roils as the World Eater's tentacles continue to dip in and out of my brother's wound. I swallow back my horror and throw my sword aside. I slam my hands against his flank.

'Take my power!' I cry. Fire and heat score through him, building and fortifying. He snarls in pain, my magic too different from his own for his body to bear with comfort. But it works. Wildcat bunches his muscles and with a sudden surge pulls free of the coiling flesh holding him prone. He roars and the rock around us shudders. Gore drips from his chest, scarlet against golden fur. His eyes blaze bright, two suns in his ruined face. He blows out his breath.

A green storm rises. Vegetation burgeons into existence, born impossibly from barren stone. Spiked vines crawl and seethe, covered in heavy purple blooms. They pin the World Eater's arms to the ground, green ropes of life and a monster's despair.

Leopard tree saplings follow the vines, trunks thickening as they gain years in moments. Yellow blooms give way to seeds and like single-winged butterflies, they break free to carry on the rank breeze.

Ah! I see! A good plan, Brother …

I grin and gather the seeds to my breast.

I warm them with my flame and whisper purpose into them. They respond. I release them and they stream upwards in a column, then fall.

The World Eater screams at their touch.

Its slimy skin chars. Wounds gape and the seeds nestle in. Roots form and burrow into the World Eater's exposed lesions. The trees grow and begin to flower. A carpet of bright yellow blooms fall to cover the stricken monster. Its tentacles fall away, consumed again by the darkness of the Line.

But something still writhes at the edge of the crevasse. A lone, severed tentacle jerks. The limb shudders again and spits black blood across the stone. Then the limb falls still. A soft blue light glows through the flesh and I know it to be soul light—the life force that belongs to all living things, the source of magic the World Eater feeds upon.

The blue light dims and the tentacle changes shape. A tuft of soft copper feathers emerges from the suckered end. Then the flesh splits into three. Wings take shape, a body. And from a face still hidden, an avian cry fills the air.

My heart shears in two …

Is it possible?

And it is. Separated from the World Eater, the tentacle has become the uncorrupted form of a summer eagle. The monster must have consumed its soul within the cleft. With a frantic beat of wings, my child tries to clear the Line. Her copper beak parts in a cry, desperate for freedom. Hands shaking, I gather my power. Chains built of heat and light circle the bird. I only need to support her long enough to break free. She cries again. Sharp. Piercing.

Almost clear.

But the World Eater rises. It's injured and no doubt wants the power of a full, true soul to heal. I clench my teeth, my muscles burn with the effort of holding my magic to bear—

But the tentacles tear the eagle from the rim. She falls away into the depths, golden feathers falling like rain in her wake.

I choke back a sob.

No mother should lose a child twice.

But grief is not new to me. Death comes with each turn of every season. And Wildcat still needs me.

My brother stands, head down, lungs heaving. Around him rustles the garden he created, a carpet of life to cover the ugliness of this battle.

'Are you all right?' I ask.

He lifts his head—his beautiful, scarred face. The weight of his existence is carried in each line.

'I am depleted, Sister,' he says. 'The fight grows harder each time I pass.'

'The World Eater is desperate.'

'Because of it, none of us are free,' says Wildcat.

'We chose this life,' I say. 'Remember?'

Wildcat looks to the sky now darkening to the deep purple that precedes the night. 'I sometimes question our wisdom. We could've left this planet.'

I frown. Has the endless battle become too much for him?

'Do you wish to turn aside from our purpose?'

Wildcat chuckles weakly; his golden teeth glitter. 'It was I who tied us to that purpose. I wanted to save Earth—to prevent what happened on our own planet from happening again.'

'Do you wish to die, then?' I ask. 'To let this world go?'

'No. My essence is life. I don't crave endings. Forgive my melancholia. My journey home stretches out long ahead and I only fear, right now, I haven't the strength to make it.'

'Then I'll help you, Brother. Rest now. The sway of seasons will be maintained. The Line will remain intact.'

It's time to leave. I place my fingers to my lips and whistle high and loud. My daughters will hear the call. As I wait, I prepare. I gather grasses and rich blooms and whisper them to be filled with warmth.

My ship arrives with the night. It emerges from the gloom, a translucent, white and silver ghost. I again create my skiff and gather up Wildcat. I carry him to the safety of the deck. There, I create a bed with the warmed foliage. He steps into it and sighs before settling with paws tucked to his ravaged chest. I nod to Krysanthe and she approaches with twin buckets of bone-white sand. I sprinkle it over my brother and watch as the grains settle into his wounds. The rents glow silver and then are healed. A new tracery of scars is left behind.

With a switch of greenery, I clean the dried blood from his coat and smooth it until it shines. My daughters gather around us as the night breeze ebbs and flows. Pollen and petals swirl like rain. Wildcat places his head down, and with a deep breath, he falls into slumber.

'Head south, Krysanthe,' I say, gaze fixed on the night horizon. 'Let's take him home.'

She nods and grips the wheel. My other daughters begin to sing and the wind rises. The sails snap, the sleds grind, and spring falls away.

Time for summer to reign again.

THE RAGE OF AUTUMN

Ruling Seasonal: Autumn Bear

Origin: Earth

'I betrayed a mortal king, but not my heart. She was his queen, but is my entire existence. Sent to the desert as punishment, I did not fear death, knowing she was by my side.'

— *Autumn Bear*

(1000 years ago)

T his is not the existence I chose for myself, this immortal duty that binds me. Summer Maiden and her brother Spring Wildcat made me. They transformed my human body into a tool to fulfil their purposes, but I have no interest in doing their bidding, in saving worlds. All I wish for is the company of my lost love—Winter Crone. When our lives were shared, her forthrightness tempered my erratic disposition. Without her, anger consumes me.

Gossamer dreams linger as I stir from hibernation, images illuminated against the dark, damp-moist rock of my cave. I imagine Winter Crone sitting at a table carved of grey ice and lined in russet brown leaves. Her dark skirts puddle like ink at her feet and her eyes, black as coal, are fixed to mine. My heart clenches. If only I could share my pain with her, explain why I possess the bodies of human children at each turn of the winter solstice to battle her. I need her to understand what I do is for love. A bid to see Crone again for just a few moments before I am forced back into slumber—just a few moments.

The dream images fragment. Crone and her table fade.

The morning light creeps into my cave, touching the glittering stalactites that weep their way to the floor. I spread my senses, noting the slow, lazy eddies of air that speak of dying summer days. Past them chirrups the crisp chorus of late season cicadas. They sing to herald my arrival—or warn of it.

I bluster out of my cave, sending dry grasses swirling. Located on the edge of the eastern forests, I have far to travel. I gather the coiling breeze to me and head west. The earth sweeps by beneath me, painted in forests and plains. All smells dry. This summer has been harsh on the land. But such is the nature of the Seasonal who rules before me: the thrice-cursed Summer Maiden—she who scorches away all beautiful things.

The western islands emerge on the horizon. My place is the eastern mountains, but I choose to dwell here in my time. These are Crone's lands and here she slumbers, deep in the earth, in the time-cycles that are not hers. I cannot speak with her, but being close tempers me. Even now, I imagine her deep, steady breaths under the warm, rich earth and the tightness in my core eases.

Singing carries on the warm air. Islander voices rise in song to guide me to their shores. The scents of roasting coconut and stewed dates curl around me— the Feast of Autumn has begun.

The ocean swells below me, a tapestry of turquoise and sapphire. Sunlight glints along the tops of cresting waves. I kiss the foam as I pass. The froth clings to my shadow, giving me ephemeral form.

A beach appears, a golden line on the horizon backed by a curtain of jungle green. I twist upwards, blowing my autumn breath across the tips of the highest trees—the jungle kings. The youngest of leaf tips shrivel instantly to brown, and the oldest wilt in their sorrow at the loss.

The voices of Islanders that worship me rise, rapturous.

'Autumn Bear! Autumn Bear! King of the Slow Death!'

I skirt the cove and land on the isolated spit of sand to the north.

Summer Maiden waits at the line where dry sand meets wet—she, the warrior goddess of the Lands behind the Sun, all gold and glitter. Perfect and alien. She holds the reins of my season in her left fist, a fist full of copper fire, which sparks and snaps and rails against its containment.

But instead of setting free the fire that gives me a semblance of form to do my season's work, she waits.

I growl low. How presumptuous. She thinks, even after all these years, she can sway my mind.

Her pale skin gleams diamond-like in the midday sun. Her golden hair coils over her bare shoulders. Eyes, the blue of summer skies, hold mine. She looks weary.

'Well met, Autumn Bear,' she says. There is no joy in her voice. We both know she tolerates my freedom only to ensure her precious prison—the Line—and the World Eater contained within it is maintained.

My freedom taken to ensure this world doesn't fall to the monster's teeth like hers did.

My presence unsettles the sand at her feet. 'Maiden.'

The breakers crash quietly behind her. Gulls cry in the distance.

'Have you found wisdom in this last turn of hibernation?' she asks.

I coil my presence tighter. 'Our ideals still differ.'

Maiden sighs. 'Please, Bear. Your pain distresses me. Let me ease it.'

'As you did for Crone when you told her she could not be with me?'

Maiden shakes her head. 'You were both dying when I found you in the desert. I gave Crone an option and she agreed to pay the price. But Bear, her choice was not made lightly. Her heart broke before she let me take her memories and the pain of losing you away.'

'I don't resent her protecting herself, but I will not forget that *I* love *her*.'

'I can't force you to let me help you, but I ask, what is gained in remaining torn?'

I growl, the sound a rumble on the wind. 'I get to remember I was once a man, and that I was loved.'

Maiden frowns. 'Your worshippers love you.'

'It's not the same.'

Maiden's gaze drops. Sunlight catches on the tips of her golden lashes. 'Had I known your heart, I would never have made you bear the burden of a Seasonal's purpose. I wouldn't have asked Spring Wildcat to change and save you on that day so long ago.'

'He didn't save us. He stole our humanity and tore our love apart. And when I defied you for that desecration, you took my physical body from me— "live forever, but not together," I think were your words.'

'I couldn't alter your fate, Bear. Wildcat's changes were absolute. Your season balanced and the guarding of the Line are all that is left for you now.'

'How can no contingency be given for love? Why must all be sacrificed to hold the world sacrosanct?'

Maiden's shoulders slump. 'Because love is for mortals. You and Crone are no longer that. This memory you cling to is just that, a memory. The fibre of your nature has changed. You think yourself capable of earthly love, but you aren't, Bear. Your emotion lingers only because you have been made to relish the slow death, to covet the last lingering of colour and warmth—that is your nature now.'

I spiral, my essence poised and pointed like a knife. 'I wasn't given a choice.'

Maiden sighs. 'What choice was there? Your mortal king had sent you both to my desert to die. At death's door, Crone in her human form, with her human frailties, chose this alternative life for you. She took my offer of immortality in return for eternal duty to this world. She did this because her love for you outweighed all else. She wanted you to live. Is that not enough?'

'No. It is not. You took her from me.'

Maiden straightens her shoulders. 'Bear, I am sorry for the rules that dictate our existence. But I promise, commit to your duty as Crone has, give me your memories, and I'll return your corporeal body and you'll find peace.'

'My memories are coin to be bartered?'

'Of course not.' Summer Maiden sighs. 'This hatred of me cannot sustain you forever. And it will never win you back Crone, only more pain.'

'It's my pain to bear. That, at least, is something you cannot control.'

'Bear, it has been centuries, and still you cling so desperately to your humanity. I ask you, do you even remember your human name?'

'Autumn Bear,' I say.

Maiden looks sad and I hesitate. Have I recalled my name incorrectly? I scan my memories. No. That is the only name I remember ever having.

'You *are* Autumn Bear. And both the bravest and most pig-headed immortal I know.'

'Your flattery means nothing to me.'

'I'm aware of that.' Maiden blinks. 'And here I am again, having failed to bend you to reason. Now my time has waned. Are you ready for your turn to balance the seasons?'

'The work must be done. They were also your terms, correct?'

'Indeed. Can I at least ask you not to fight Winter Crone when your time ends?'

'You cannot stop me seeing her.'

'I only wish to stop you from hurting her.'

I bluster, setting Maiden's curls to dancing. 'Not to hurt her, Maiden. Never that. I fight her because it makes her hate me—makes her feel … something … at least, for me. It's a fine line between love and hate. One day she'll win free of your spell, even just for a moment, and remember who I am. And for that moment, she will love me again. I'll bear all the pain in the world for that single hope. I will not stop fighting.'

Maiden sighs and the temperature drops. She nods and then lifts her fist. The copper fire in her hand unravels and, like a storm of sparks, settles around me. Where they touch my incorporeal form, they blossom into leaf-shaped light. I begin to resolve, my shadowy body built of russet leaves and threads of copper light.

Not enough of a corporeal figure to search for Crone in her earthly den, but just enough to reach out and touch the trees and stroke the earth towards winter.

In the distance, the Islanders' song grows louder. They call me. I smile. Their love is not the same as Crone's once was, but it fills a small cavern in my heart.

I turn back to Maiden but she has disappeared. Sea foam and soldier crabs scuttle in the impressions her feet left in the sand.

I take a deep breath. I have work to do and preparations to make.

Soon it will be time to try and win back my Winter Crone again.

CRONE AND THE GIRL

WINTER

Ruling Seasonal: Winter Crone

Origin: Earth

'A hole resides where my heart should be—an emptiness. I don't know why this bothers me. I'm not a Seasonal to love or be loved. I am wrought of ice, not fire. Only frost and death flow through my veins.'

— *Winter Crone*

(Current year)

Crone

Music coils in ice and upon the fall of midnight moonlight—the song of autumn as it bleeds its final breaths into winter. Worms tumble away from my ragged, black skirts as I rise from the roots of the oldest tree. The Father. I suck in the cold-sharpened air and the heady scent of his pine needles. They fill my lungs. I relish the knife-keen sensation.

My turn has come.

Time to lay bare the bones of this world.

My limbs gain strength as my earth-clogged arteries shift to flesh and blood begins to flow. I move into the clearing. The glade of half-shadows and clover responds to my presence, freezing over. Surfaces sparkle, bespeckled in jewels of newly formed frost. Twelve sentinel trees—Sons to the Father—circle the grove. They stand with bristling green heads bent low and rugged shoulders hung heavy with my hoarfrost.

The sons do not love me as their father does. Still young, they despise the coldness of my touch. They do not understand that three months of winter beget nine months of life.

If only there were a way to soften my touch and teach the living to love the cold.

I release my breath, one that carries both the scent of frost and carrion. I am cursed by my nature to be lonely. But at least I have purpose and that must be made to be enough.

***

Girl

I awoke this morning with a bear on my back.

He rode the last of the autumn winds to claim me.

This turn of the season, I am his chosen warrior.

Crone rises from the base of Father Tree and steps into the circle of moonlight. Debris tumbles away to reveal a clean, pale woman—a half-woman. The trembling light catches the lines of her ice-feathered face, her cruel black eye with its wicked, cold gleam and long dark teeth. Her breath blooms, as white as her skin. It clouds the light, fouling the air with the stench of damp earth and death.

I crouch, my hand pressed to the rough trunk of the closest sentinel tree. I sense nothing from it. No quiet presence to ease my anxiety. I swallow. No time to fear. I am here to honour my people—here to save them from the ravages of winter.

I squeeze the hilt of the knife sheathed at my side. It is the blade my father forbade me to bring. His voice fills my mind.

'I would speak to you of destiny, child. Would say you were born for this.' His black eyes flick to the bear mark I awoke to find staining my skin this morning—on this day of the winter solstice. The orange and russet colour of it marks my throat, creeps across my shoulder to disappear down my back.

'But it would be a falsehood,' he says. 'I do not see why Autumn Bear chose you. Only half of you belongs to this land—half is of my bloodline. You are cursed.'

'But I am your daughter.'

'Defeat Crone and honour our lord Bear and then you may call yourself such. Until then you are nothing to me.'

No love lost between father and daughter.

My mother is Serina. She gifted me the knife. She slipped it beneath my pillow and whispered in my ear.

'No child of mine will be sent to battle without a weapon.'

Such is the sentiment of a Daughter born to the warrior tribes who dwell over the sea and behind the sun—the place where Summer Maiden reigns.

But my mother is also a slave wife; one of ten claimed by my Island Chieftain father. Red-haired and blue-eyed, she is by far the most distinctive and most defiant. Before her time here, she roamed desert oceans and distant seas in a glass and whale-skin ship, a captain in service to the Maiden. She was captured when her vessel shattered its bones against the coast of this island and her crew perished.

***

Crone

I smell her. Girl with Bear Riding Her Back. Her scent is peppery, a mix of the familiar Islander bloodline and something else I half recall but cannot place. What is that coursing through her blood? It holds heat.

I snort away the stench. There is nothing to fear. Bear and his chosen ones always fall to the bitter length of my claws.

Winter always prevails.

Girl steps clear of the tree. The stained skin on her throat, my enemy's mark, seethes in the uncertain light. She is wiry and strong, a good companion for Bear—the Autumn Soldier whose nature is of slow deaths, of savagery and brutal instincts.

I unsheathe my ebony claws. Girl's eyes, blue as glacier ice, lock to them and widen. But she stands resolute. She comes willingly to the fight. No fear fills her. She is a female with strength of character. A quality I respect.

But strength is not everything.

Winter is inevitable.

Girl slides forward. Dressed in hunting leathers, she moves cleanly. Her light brown hair, tied in a tail, hangs stick-straight down her back. Her skin is paler than most Bear chooses to face me. And those eyes—

Not Islander eyes.

One step, two steps. Frozen grass snaps beneath her fish leather boots. She stumbles but her step corrects. I sense the shift in her, of a change from human to animal. Her shoulders hunch. Her chin lifts.

Defiant.

Bear has claimed her.

As my enemy asserts himself over the mind of Girl, I pity her. Disappointment rages like a butterfly trapped behind her gaze. But this is how it always is. Bear's chosen, like Father and his sons, will stand as witness to the battle, but nothing more.

This battle of Winter Crone and Autumn Bear.

Girl's features crinkle into a wrinkle-nosed snarl. Bear's voice claims her throat.

'We meet again, Crone,' he growls.

'It *is* solstice,' I reply.

Bear smiles a wicked smile. Girl's blunt-edged, human teeth are at odds with the feral fire of Bear's presence within her.

'I am not ready to relinquish my claim.'

I sigh. 'You never are, Bear.'

***

Girl

I watch but cannot control. Our minds are linked. I know the truth. Bear has claimed my body for he lost his long ago in a skirmish against—or was it for?— Crone. His thoughts are muddled. But either way, it was a bitter defeat and the reason he now claims children like me to fight his battles.

Shared vision reveals all details, flash point clean. Crone—she glides across the ground, a trail of ice following in her wake. Bear—he roars, setting my teeth to trembling and ears to ringing. He curls my fingers and considers how my human nails are blunt and ineffectual. I sense his wish for claws, to gut and gore. But he will make do with what he has. I visualize the knife in the sheath at my belt. His hope flares. He understands. Then the weapon is cold against my palm.

A single silver claw.

Better than none.

Crone screeches, the sound so piercing my heart almost stops. Her black teeth grind like ice over stone. She leaps the last few steps to lock freezing hands around my throat. Bear swipes, and our knife's edge slices Crone's forearm. She hisses as blood, crystal clear, fans out against the moonlight. Her grip slips.

Crone glides back and turns to the sentinel trees. 'He cheats! He bears fire-forged steel.'

But the sons remain stoic. No help will be given from that quarter.

She turns to Father Tree. He too stands silent, his roots dug too deep to move and his voice not made for either mortal or immortal ears to hear.

Crone turns in a sweep of skirts. A glimmer of fear touches the old woman's eyes.

'Like me, you are a Seasonal, Bear. Your duty is to protect this world. But instead, you wish to keep your season eternal? If you do this, the natural balance will fail. Without me, Earth cannot rest and rejuvenate. Spring Wildcat will never waken to walk and seed new plants with his breath; Summer Maiden's Line—that great crevasse that holds imprisoned the most terrible monsters of this world—will open. They'll consume everything. Time will stop. You will stop. All will end.'

Bear's voice is guttural and black. 'I care not for the Line, for Spring Wildcat, nor Summer Maiden, only Autumn Bear.'

'If you win today, so comes the end of days.'

'No,' whispers Bear, 'the world will endure.'

But Bear is lying. I sense it. He knows she speaks the truth. He just doesn't care. His desires rule him.

A chill crawls through my soul. I assess Crone—peer into the deepness of her eyes, past the terror of her claws and teeth and the smell of her breath. And there the truth is revealed. She is not the enemy. She understands her place and knows that change must always balance the cycle of days.

Bear cannot be allowed to win.

But what can I do, trapped as I am?

Crone glides forward again and strikes. Her claws catch and tear my skin. I sob as blood flows down my neck but the sound never leaves my mouth. Bear's voice answers. His howl of pain and frustration rocks the clearing. Pine needles from Father Tree's branches fall as green rain.

Bear cares nothing for the damage to my body. He cares nothing for me. Instead, he gathers the final strength left to my limbs and advances. His roar rocks the clearing again; Crone stumbles before the force of it but rights herself. She bares her teeth and slithers forward, viper-fast and shadow-thin.

More blood is lost. And heat.

Then the smell of ash surrounds me.

I blink as the wounds on my neck begin to burn. My blood erupts into fire, turning from scarlet to shining gold as it seeps across my torso. Then it boils. Fetid steam rises to cloud my vision—or more so Bear's vision. He halts.

'What is this?'

A cackling laugh fills the air, slow at first but rising to a crescendo.

The steam clears.

Crone is kneeling in the dirt, ragged skirts crumpled around her. Her dark eyes fix on Bear.

'Couldn't smell it in her blood, could you?' she says.

Fear fills Bear. My heart soars with hope.

'Of what do you speak?' he replies.

'Your chosen one. She is Islander by birth but also part Daughter from the Lands behind the Sun. The fire in her blood is your undoing.'

The mark on my shoulder writhes. The skin on my back blisters. I reel with pain but cannot act. The stench of scorched flesh fills the air and Bear whimpers.

'Summer Maiden? She's coming? Intervening?'

'Yes,' laughs Crone. 'You wielded *her* fire-forged steel against me with a stolen hand. Hold witness now as you are pulled from the flesh.'

Bear screams as his essence is torn from my body. Released, I fall to my knees, limbs wooden and bloodless. I look up. A rusty, bear-shaped shadow hovers before me. Behind it stands a glowing woman, tresses of gold cascading over her naked breasts.

'I will not let you hurt Crone, Bear' she says, her voice sparking embers from clear air.

'You have no right to stop me,' he snarls, his voice whisper thin.

Summer Maiden frowns. 'But I must. Your season has ended. Now it's her time to reign.'

Maiden pushes the shadow with her slim-fingered hand. Bear dissipates, lost in a sudden flurry of orange, red, and umber leaves.

I look to the sky. Have the stars darkened or the moon faded? I can't be sure, but everything seems dimmed. Cold seeps from the ground into my legs and for the first time, I am afraid. I am dying. The sentinel trees and their father loom over me, bristling shadows against a darker night. Only Summer Maiden burns bright as she leans over me. Her eyes, like blue embers, catch mine. Her fingers brush my forehead. 'I'm sorry, child,' she whispers.

Crone approaches, her skirts murmuring.

'Is there nothing you can do?' she asks. 'Her kin are of your realm.'

Summer Maiden frowns. 'I would but her blood is thinned. Half belongs to this place. She would burn in my kingdom if I took her there.'

Crone swallows. The lines of her face deepen, and her cheek glistens with frost.

'Would you permit her to join me?'

The maiden's eyes widen. 'Are you lonely?'

'No,' says Crone. 'But I have need of her. This child has heart. I've seen it. She could convince the humans to no longer worship Bear and instead tolerate me—teach them to love winter.'

Summer Maiden turns back to me. 'What do you say, Girl? If we save your life, will you apprentice yourself to Crone? Would you speak for winter to your kin?'

I have no wish to die. And the importance of Crone's purpose is clear to me. My throat is too dry to answer so I nod.

Yes.

Crone reaches down. Her touch is cold fire on my shoulder. But soon the pain of my scorched skin eases. The wounds on my neck heal.

'Are you ready, Girl?' asks Crone. 'Winter cannot wait forever.'

I get to my feet. I turn my hands over. My skin has changed. It now sparkles white and silver, covered in a layer of ice just like Crone's. I stretch my fingers and feel the press of new claws aching to extend.

'I am ready,' I say.

Crone lifts her hands. A bitter wind builds in her palms, cold enough to bring aches to bone. Then she sends it forth in a torrent to cover the land and sea. It blisters past me with a screech, whipping my hair to snarls. The temperature drops as ice crystals form in flurries. Summer Maiden wraps her arms around herself and disappears in a puddle of light. The island groans as ice and snow settle across it. Crone smiles.

'Now we find your kin,' she says. 'And speak with your father.'

'He won't listen,' I say. 'The chieftain despises me.'

Crone bares her wicked, sharp teeth. There is kindness in her heart, but also a hard coldness born inherently of her nature. 'Then we crown someone else. Shall we give your mother his throne? Could she love us?'

'She would.'

'Then come.' Crone grasps my hand. Together, we leap into the air. The freezing wind catches and carries us toward the coast and toward my tribe.

As we fly, music coils in the ice below us and upon the fall of midnight moonlight.

About the Author

Pamela Jeffs is a speculative-fiction author living in Queensland, Australia with her husband and two daughters. Her work has been published previously in various magazines and anthologies, both nationally and internationally, and has been shortlisted for multiple awards, including numerous Australian *Aurealis Awards* and *Ditmar Awards,* and has been twice noted in the *Writers of the Future Competition.*

Prior to pursuing her passion for writing, Pamela's background was in interior and exhibition design. This allowed her to collaborate with a multitude of talented artists and designers across a number of artistic platforms.

The Seasonals is her fifth collection.

To discover more books by Pamela Jeffs and be notified of new releases, deals, and specials, visit and subscribe at:

www.pamelajeffs.com
Twitter: @Pamela_Jeffs
Facebook: @pamelajeffsauthor

OTHER TITLES

Discover other titles by Pamela Jeffs at:
www.pamelajeffs.com

Including:

<u>Collections</u>

Red Hour and Other Strange Tales
Saloons & Stardust: A Collection
Five Dragons
The Terralight Collection
Turtle Island

<u>Co-Authored Anthologies</u>

The Zookeeper's Tales of Interstellar Oddities

If you enjoyed this book, please go to Goodreads
and/or Amazon and leave a review. It helps
Thank you.